LIKE FATHER, NOT LIKE SONS

BY

Eidahs

COVER BY
BINKY INK

BINKY INK

THE LITERARY ARM OF BINKY PRODUCTIONS

WWW.BINKYPRODUCTIONS.COM/SHORT STORIES

Published in 2024 by Binky Ink

ISBN: 978-1-7382829-0-6

Table of Contents

Part 1: Eliminate

Simon entered the bar, walking straight over to the counter where Rita, his friend and barmaid, was cleaning glasses. The sun had just barely set and Simon was glad to see the place wasn't too busy. He needed a quiet one.

'Evening, boss,' said Rita.

Simon hissed a laugh. 'How many times do I have to tell you not to call me "boss" just because I own this bar? I'm half your age.'

'Don't say that too loud,' Rita chided playfully. 'Most patrons think I'm at least a dozen years younger than I actually am.'

'You're certainly a fit woman,' Simon complimented her. She blushed and playfully slapped him with her cloth. Simon chuckled.

Only then did Simon notice the man sitting at the back of the bar in a dim corner at a single table, slowly sipping a drink. Simon tensed.

'How long has he been here?' he growled.

'Been there almost all day,' replied Rita. 'Been ordering lots, tips generously. You know him?'

'Unfortunately, I do.'

Simon strode over to the table where the man five years his senior sat and pulled the chair across from him loudly. Simon sat down and leaned towards the other man.

'What the hell are you doing here, Johnny?' he growled harshly.

'Good to see you too, Simon.'

Simon balled his hands into fists. 'I'll ask again, what are you doing in my bar?'

'Staking out,' Johnny replied, his voice low.

Simon narrowed his eyes and studied Johnny's face for a few minutes. 'No phone call, no letter, no email, no nothing *for ten years—*'

'And whose fault is that?' retorted Johnny. 'I couldn't find you.'

'You obviously did at some point, else you wouldn't be here. Or did you just find me now?' Johnny downcast his eyes and Simon knew the answer to his question was no.

'Look, I'm not here to cause trouble, I'm here to make sure it doesn't come to you.'

'What the hell are you talking about, Johnny? Trouble?'

'Simon, please, I'm on your side here!' pleaded Johnny.

'My side? You chose your side when you stayed with dad,' Simon spat back.

'I thought I could change him,' admitted Johnny. 'I was wrong. He left and disappeared shortly after you and mom moved upstate.'

'He beat ma,' Simon sneered through gritted teeth.

'I know,' insisted Johnny. 'I thought I could make him see . . . I was wrong. I'm sorry.'

'So what?' Simon leaned back in his seat, folding his arms across his chest. 'You say he left. Then why didn't you come find us to tell us, huh?'

Johnny opened his mouth to answer and then his eyes darted to the door and he straightened. Simon turned to follow his gaze, only to find Salazar, a local gang leader, thief, and criminal, enter the bar with his lackeys.

Ever since Salazar had arrived in this town, he'd been making trouble for the locals and for Simon's business.

Simon slowly stood from his seat and walked over to where Salazar was already heckling Rita.

'Something I can help you with, Salazar?' Simon demanded condescendingly. 'Only you seem to forget I barred you from ever returning to my bar.'

'You think you make the law around here?' sneered Salazar.

'In my establishment, yes.' Simon didn't back down. 'Now, I'll only ask this of you once: Leave.'

'That's not going to happen,' replied Salazar. 'You're going to give me what I want.'

Simon grinned sinisterly. 'That's not going to happen. I paid for this place. I ain't giving the deeds away to some bozo.'

'Is that so?'

Simon saw Salazar flick a knife from his wrist. He froze, calculating what to do next.

From across the bar, an ashtray hit Salazar's hand and the criminal dropped his knife, cursing. Simon looked over to where Johnny now stood, hands poised for a fight.

'You pull a knife on him and it's over, Salazar.' Johnny's warning was commanding and threatening. Salazar narrowed his eyes at Johnny.

Simon's eyes darted from Salazar to Johnny, observing how they reacted to each other. Salazar bent to pick up his knife and Johnny leapt over the table, bounded over and kicked Salazar in the chest, sending him to the ground and training a gun on him.

'End of the line, Salazar. I'm taking you in and you're going to answer some questions.'

'Taking him in? Staking out?' breathed Simon. 'God damn it, Johnny! You're—' He pressed his lips to a thin line and breathed out angrily.

'Sorry, Simon,' Johnny answered, never taking his eyes off Salazar. 'That's why I couldn't reach out. I've been hunting someone for a long time and—' Johnny took a step forward as Salazar twitched. 'Hands on your head, Salazar. Now!'

Salazar swept a kick to Johnny's hands and the gun went flying across the bar.

'Shit!' Johnny cursed.

Salazar got to his feet as one of his subordinates grabbed hold of Johnny from behind, who expertly swung a fist backwards into his attacker's face and the lackey staggered back, nose bloodied.

Simon took a few steps back as Rita bent behind the counter.

Someone grabbed Simon from behind him and pulled him to the ground. Simon punched his opponent in the gut only to be flipped over flat on his stomach, arms twisted painfully behind his back.

Simon's attacker placed a knife to his throat. Simon gasped, heart hammering in his chest with the fear his attacker had elicited within him.

'Detective John Miller!' the man pinning Simon down called out.

Johnny whipped his head, his eyes landing on Simon, and he froze in place. A hush fell over the bar. Salazar snickered and sauntered over towards him, flicking his knife menacingly.

'I don't know who this loser is to you,' began Salazar, 'but I'll have him killed if you— '

'Over my dead body,' seethed Johnny.

Two gunshots broke the eerie stillness of the moment. Simon saw Salazar fall back, clutching his thigh, just as the man pinning Simon dropped heavily on top of him; the hand holding the knife went limp.

The door at the back burst open and several armed officers poured into the bar, weapons trained on Salazar and his lackeys. The head criminal groaned, lamenting his predicament.

Simon shoved the dead henchman off him and got to his hands and knees, tentatively stretching out his neck and feeling it for any injuries. That had been too close.

Someone in the shadows twitched and lunged forward. Simon glanced at the ground, following the man's trajectory, and saw Johnny's gun. He kicked it over to Johnny and away from the criminal. His brother expertly bent forward, grabbed the gun, spun, and with a click, pressed it against the attacking man's back as Johnny bent him over the counter.

'I recommend you cease all movement and put your hands on your head,' Johnny condescended.

The criminal sheepishly placed his hands on his head and the other officers handcuffed Salazar and his team before proceeding to drag them out of the bar.

A tall older man walked up to Johnny. 'Well done, Miller. Hopefully, we're one step closer to catching our guy.'

'Hopefully,' muttered Johnny. He approached Simon. 'Listen, I owe you one hell of an explana—'

Simon's fist struck Johnny's jaw, sending him careening sideways. Johnny placed a hand on his jaw, mouth agape.

'Hey, you just assaulted—'

'Graham!' Johnny held up his hand to stop the older officer. 'No, he didn't.' He turned back to face Simon. 'He assaulted his brother. And I suppose I deserved that.'

'Yeah, you did. And yeah, you do owe me an explanation.' Simon clenched his jaw and unclenched it.

'Look, now that I don't have to . . .' Johnny paused. 'I'd like us to stay in touch.'

'You have one hour,' declared Simon. 'Then I decide if we stay in touch or not.'

'I need you to make a statement, Mr . . . Simon Miller, I gather?' the older man said.

Simon looked from him and back to his brother. 'Fine. I'll make the statement.' He leaned forward on one leg. 'Then you have an hour to tell me what the hell is going on.'

Johnny nodded.

Simon walked over to the officer taking statements, who addressed the older officer as Chief Officer Graham. The guy asked Simon several questions but it didn't take too long. Some of the questions threw him off guard, and Simon glared at Johnny suspiciously, angry at his brother for abandoning him in the first place when Simon was just fifteen.

He walked back to Johnny. 'Talk, now.' Johnny nodded slowly. 'And why was that guy asking me about our dad?'

Johnny sighed. 'That's who I'm hunting.'

'What?' Simon breathed, his voice dangerously low.

Johnny looked around. 'After you and mom got away, he tried to rope me into his schemes. We had a fight – a literal fistfight. Then he left. That's when I decided I'd stop him. I got into the academy, but my affiliation with a wanted criminal . . .' His brows creased with chagrin. 'I felt ashamed for deserting you and mom. By the time I was ready to reach out, I was set to hunt him and had to keep all communication with you . . . well, "cease" all communication.' Johnny made air quotes.

Simon crossed his arms, leaning back on the bar counter. 'There was no communication *to begin with.*'

'He's a wanted criminal, Simon. He's killed a lot of people.'

'And Salazar?'

'Works for him. When I found out, we followed Salazar's operations and took our investigation here. I insisted I be the one to deal with Salazar.' Johnny passed a hand over his face. 'I knew it wouldn't be safe with dad on the loose, so I convinced my supervising officer to station undercover cops here to keep you safe.'

Simon let that sink in. He shrugged. 'Thanks, I guess.'

'With Salazar in custody, we've eliminated one of dad's largest gangs and supply sources to trafficked weapons.'

Simon worked his jaw, unsure what to make of his brother's confession.

'Look, is there a place where we can talk more privately?' asked Johnny.

'Yeah. I still live with ma. She needed help after her accident. Did you know about it?'

'You received a generous donation for her operation, did you not?' asked Johnny.

Simon hissed. 'That was you?'

Johnny nodded. 'I'm sorry, Simon. I did you and mom wrong.'

Simon sighed. He shook his head. 'No, I under-stand. I get it. I just wish you'd reached out sooner.'

'I know.'

'Come.'

Simon led Johnny to a small apartment building not too far from the bar. They walked up the steps to the apartment and entered the place.

'Hey, ma,' Simon called out as they walked through the dim corridor to the living room. 'Guess who finally showed his face again?'

Simon and Johnny both froze when they saw their mother tied to a chair, hands bound behind her back, and mouth gagged with cloth. Behind her, stood a familiar strong-built man in the same hat and trenchcoat he'd always worn, holding a gun.

'Guess who finally showed his face again, indeed.' The man sneered, stepping into the light of the lamp. He grinned. 'Hello, boys. Welcome to this much-awaited family reunion.'

Part 2: Knowledge

John tensed and held his breath. This was not how he'd hoped things would go down. Next to him, he heard Simon swallow loudly.

'Hello, dad,' John breathed, his breath shaking. 'I've been hunting you for a long time.'

'As I've been hunting you, son.'

Simon remained petrified, staring jaw clenched at their mother whose eyes were pleading, her face streaked with tears.

John pressed his lips into a thin line. He had tried so hard to keep them safe. But his father, just like he'd been all thirty years of John's life, was one step ahead and ready to do the unthinkable.

John cursed himself internally. He had his earpiece in his ear still, but he had switched it off after the altercation at his brother's bar. He needed a way to switch it back on without arousing suspicion, without tipping his father off.

His father was like any other criminal he'd taken down, though – he had to remind himself. He had to get him off his guard to get the upper hand. To do that, he had to find out what made him tick. And to find that, he had to keep him talking. Knowledge was key.

John considered reaching for his gun and realized he should have done so the moment they had walked in.

The muzzle of a gun pressed against John's temple as someone behind him stepped towards him and unclipped his gun, tossing it towards his father. Someone else held a gun to Simon's temple. Their father's lackeys, a man behind John, by what he could gather, and a woman behind Simon, were smirking.

'Now, sit, boys. Let's catch up.'

John had to keep his nerves in check, allowing his breathing to keep his heart from beating out of his chest completely. He saw Simon wasn't faring so well. Without the training John had received, he reckoned he'd be in an even worse state than his brother was.

Their father's subordinates shoved Simon and John to some chairs and sat them down, binding their hands behind the backs of the chairs. The rope was brittle, it splintered and burned, but John knew how to get himself out of it – if he was careful and worked slowly. Getting to his gun was another story.

Their father turned to them. 'Now, let's talk about that disappointment of a son I have who decided to betray me and became, what is it, an agent, detective?'

'Detective John Miller, Mr. Miller,' John replied professionally. 'I'm sorry you saw it as a betrayal, dad, but at the end of the day, Tyler Miller is just another criminal.'

'Oh, is that how you see it, Johnny? After everything I did for you?' Tyler took a menacing step forward.

'You mean after you tried to make me kill a man who beat you up for fucking up his wife?' John glared at his father, seething. 'You raped her! When I found out and told you I let the man go, you raised your fists at me and tried to strangle me to death. So, sorry for betraying you after you disappeared to run away from the cops. But those cops trained me to hunt the very man I promised myself I wouldn't take after.' John spat on the ground.

Tyler Miller backhanded John, the elaborate rings on his fingers scratching the skin off his face. John felt blood trickle from the gash on his cheek as it stung.

'I tried to make a real man out of you, boy!' Tyler bellowed. John again had to remind himself that this man was Tyler Miller, a criminal, despite the fact that he'd conceived him and then raised him for two-thirds of his life.

'Were you just waiting for me to show my face here?' demanded John. 'Because I did everything to keep Simon and our mother safe from you.'

'*You* found them easily,' replied Tyler. 'So did I.' He glanced back at their mother who whimpered under his stare. He turned back to face John. 'Salazar tipped me off regarding a Detective Miller going after the gangs.' He chuckled mirthlessly. 'Miller. I knew it was you right away.'

'I still took down Poplevski at the water resort,' retorted John, 'and the Greenhouse operation, and let's not forget the ski resort, all operating under your control. Oh, and Salazar tonight.' John grinned tauntingly at his father.

Tyler stepped forward and thrust his gun to John's cheek, the cold metal pressing hard on the bleeding gash. 'You done gloating, son?'

John swallowed and breathed out carefully, quelling his emotions . . . and his thundering heart. So failure made his father tick, but it also made him more dangerous. 'Yes, father,' he half-whispered.

Behind Tyler, his mother began screaming into her gag. Tyler spun to face her. 'Shut up, bitch!' He hit her on the head with the butt of his gun and her head lolled forward.

'Don't!' shouted Simon but it was too late, their mother was unconscious.

'And you, Simon,' seethed Tyler, turning back to his two sons, 'abandoning your family with your mother. Running away. The great escape, was it? I knew exactly where you ran off to. If it hadn't been for your brother's friends in the police force, I would have arranged this family reunion a lot sooner.'

Simon glanced warily at John but said nothing.

'At least my other two children didn't abandon or betray me,' Tyler said after a time.

John and Simon snapped their heads to each other; Simon's face reflected John' shock. John slowly turned back to look up at his father who still loomed before him.

'What other children?' demanded John.

Tyler grinned. He motioned towards the man and the woman who stood behind John and Simon. 'Why them, of course.' He chuckled. 'Looks like Detective Miller didn't find out everything about those working for dear old Daddy Miller.'

Tyler took a beat, his grin never faltering. 'Meet your half-brother and half-sister, boys, Blake and Alia.'

Part 3: Beginning

Simon let it all sink in, slowly realizing just how much his brother had risked his life for him and their mother, just how much Johnny had done to keep them safe from their criminal father, let alone what he'd suffered at his hands. Simon realized Johnny hadn't picked the wrong side, he had just needed to stay away to keep them safe.

Simon looked over at Johnny, suddenly over-whelmed with grief, and he blinked back tears. Johnny noticed and his expression softened. Simon wanted to reach over to him but, bound as they were, all he could do was bow his head and hope his brother knew he was forgiven.

Simon looked up at their father. The man with the strong build, whose neck muscles and veins bulged, smiled sinisterly, and the man who stood behind Johnny, Blake, and the woman behind Simon, Alia, laughed condescendingly.

'So when did this happen?' Simon asked carefully. 'I reckon I'm the youngest of all siblings.'

'You are,' replied Tyler. 'I reckon I should start from the beginning. Before I met your bitch of a mother—'

'Don't call her that!' demanded Johnny.

'Careful, boy, you're in no position to make any demands here,' warned Tyler. He took a few paces and started over. 'Before I met your *bitch of a mother*,' he added extra emphasis on the insult, 'I had some fun with some whores. Alia is the eldest and deserves only respect. She found me after her mother had told her the name of her father, and when she learnt who I was, she wanted in. She was thirteen when she joined me, and has been an important member of my operations since. She is a leader in her own right.'

'You're too kind, father,' Alia said. 'It's only because I learnt from you.' Tyler smiled warmly at Alia.

Simon hissed. He must've been five if not younger when Alia joined their father, and Simon realized just how far back his father's schemes dated.

Then, his expression growing sterner, Tyler continued. 'Your half-brother, Blake, was in the system and ran into some of my men during one of our operations. I was getting ready to beat the pulp out of him when I saw his name was Blake Miller. Can you believe his mother gave him my name? And I wasn't even in the picture!' Tyler chuckled.

'The look of shock on your face when you asked me my mother's name,' Blake laughed, 'was priceless.'

Blake moved to stand in front of Simon and Johnny. 'He told me who he was and asked if I wanted to continue by his side.' He grinned. 'I got the gang I was a part of who rivaled him to join him.'

'I was so proud of you that day,' Tyler praised.

'Like father like son, then,' muttered Johnny.

'Unlike my two failures of sons – you two,' snapped Tyler.

Johnny looked over at Simon, and Simon recognized something in his eyes.

'Father,' said Alia, glancing at her phone before pocketing it. 'I've just received word that the coast is clear.'

Tyler nodded. 'We move out.' He glanced behind him. 'Alia, grab their mother, will you? Blake, take Simon. I've got Johnny.'

Blake came up behind Simon and hurled him to his feet by the neck of his shirt. Simon obliged as the other man shoved him forward.

Simon tried to glance behind at Johnny. His brother stumbled forward, resisting, and Tyler shoved him against the wall. Johnny's head hit the wall hard. He cried out.

Then Johnny's hands came free of the bonds and he sidestepped, bringing the cord up and around Tyler's neck, shoving him against the wall and strangling him. Tyler croaked a complaint.

'I've been waiting a long time to get back at you for what you did to me, Tyler Miller!' Johnny growled.

Tyler kicked backwards but Johnny moved in time, pulling harder on the grip he had around Tyler's neck.

Blake shoved Simon aside, pulling out his gun and aiming it at Johnny and fired – the shot tore through Johnny's abdomen.

'Johnny!' cried Simon.

Johnny's eyes widened in shock and he let go of Tyler as blood spilled from the wound. He pressed his hands to his ribs, wincing in pain. Tyler kicked Johnny in the face and Johnny fell onto his back. Blake and Alia were on top of him and binding his hands again. He screamed in pain and Simon could see the blood drench his brother's shirt.

Fear gripping him, Simon rushed to his brother's side, still bound and unable to help but just wanting him to know he was there.

Tyler grabbed Simon by the hair and yanked him up as Blake pulled Johnny to his feet. Johnny's breathing was heavy and gruff.

'Johnny?' Simon quavered.

'I've had worse,' Johnny managed.

Tyler barked into his phone. 'I need backup!'

A few tense moments later, with the only sound being Johnny's heavy breathing, three more of Tyler's lackeys arrived. They led Johnny and Simon down the stairs of the apartment and out the back door. They shoved them into the back of a black van.

Johnny collapsed to the floor of the van, wheezing. Blake pushed Simon – the youngest Miller landed on his side beside Johnny, who was beginning to look paler by the minute. Simon gulped in fear as the van doors shut and the van started off.

Part 4: Quiet

The pain John felt was excruciating. He'd had worse injuries, but if the gunshot wound wasn't treated soon, he would lose enough blood to lose consciousness and then eventually die. He was acutely aware of Tyler's henchwoman who stood guard over them, so John had to be careful what he said.

At least his earpiece was switched back on now. He didn't know if anyone could hear him – they had probably closed everything up – but it was worth the attempt to get backup.

Simon lay on his side next to John who lay flat on his stomach. His brother glanced down at the blood that pooled on the van's floor. He seemed mesmerized by it and terrified at the same time. John had to admit, he was feeling pretty terrified as well. If he didn't calm his nerves, his racing heart would pump all his blood out through his wound.

'Simon,' John whispered. Simon tore his eyes away from the blood and met John's gaze. 'I'm sorry, you know.'

Simon stared at him for a moment. 'I know,' he said at last.

'I'm your older brother. I wanted to protect you.' All John had *ever* wanted to do was protect his brother. 'I did you wrong, though.'

Aside from the humming of the van, it was quiet, as was it on the other end of John's earpiece.

'It's okay, Johnny.'

'I didn't want this. I didn't want it to end like this, Simon.' John felt the trickle of a tear run from his eyes, Simon's eyes also sparkled with tears. John heaved shakily.

'There a reason this is still on?' came Chief Officer Graham's voice from the other end of John's earpiece.

'The reason,' John began forcefully, 'I never reached out to you, Simon, is because I feared our father would come after you. I thought perhaps he didn't know where you were, that you'd be safe. *I was wrong.*'

'Detective Miller, is that you? What's going on? Do you read me?'

'I thought that as a detective I could catch Tyler Miller before he found me.' John's breathing was becoming more strained and he could feel his eyes flutter. He needed to stay conscious just a little bit longer.

'Miller?' Graham's voice was one of worry and uncertainty.

'Now here I am, bound, and bleeding to death in Tyler Miller's van, having failed to protect you, Simon.'

John heard Graham bark orders to the others. 'Detective Miller's been taken captive by Tyler Miller. Simon Miller's with him. Get the medics! Detective Miller's injured!'

John let out a mirthless laugh. It was done, Graham knew. They'd find them, hopefully before it was too late.

'It's okay, Johnny,' wept Simon. 'We'll find a way through this. Like when we were kids and hid from dad.'

'Shut up already!' shouted Tyler's lackey.

John jerked his head, stopping himself from nodding off.

'Johnny, Johnny, stay with me. Okay? Just stay with me.' Simon stared at John, fear in his eyes.

'All I wanted to do was protect you and mom,' whispered Johnny.

Simon shut his eyes and a tear poured down the side of his face to the floor. John felt himself tremble as fogginess overtook his mind. He blinked, willing himself to remain conscious.

'Simon,' he whispered. 'You're right. It's going to be okay.'

Everything around John grew quiet; Graham's voice in his earpiece was muffled, and Simon's lips were moving but John was unable to make out what

he was saying. John smiled at Simon as his eyes
fluttered and darkness overtook him.

PART 5: CHANGES

'Johnny? Johnny, come on, stay with me. Johnny!'

'Shut up!' the woman complained.

Simon stared at Johnny's unconscious form during the entire trip, a lump in his throat. Trepidation overtook him – he was convinced he was going to die.

The van stopped and Simon's heart skipped a beat. The door to the back of the van opened and Tyler loomed like a shadow against the beam of light that came from the warehouse behind him. Simon squinted, his eyes hurting from the sudden light.

Tyler barked orders to Alia and Blake who grabbed Simon and Johnny.

'He's lost consciousness! Careful!' protested Simon as Alia grabbed Johnny.

She looked over at Tyler.

'Check him,' Tyler instructed.

Alia nodded once and checked that Johnny wasn't faking. He wasn't, Simon knew he wasn't. Alia then checked his pulse.

'Pulse is weak, father. Should we just end him now?'

Simon's protest caught in his throat and instead his entire body convulsed with tremors of fear.

Tyler sighed loudly, looking over at Blake. 'You just had to shoot him.'

'What? He had one over on you!' insisted Blake.

Tyler waved a hand dismissively. 'Get him upstairs anyway. We'll inject him with some stimulants. I want him awake for the big moment.'

Simon swallowed hard. He didn't know what that entailed but he certainly didn't like the sound of it.

Alia got behind him and pushed him forward, pressing her gun to his back. 'Try anything and you're dead, boy, you hear me?'

Simon nodded, gulping down the sick feeling he had, and he staggered forward, following his father up the stairs to a large loft.

Blake let Johnny drop to the floor with a loud thud. Simon jerked in place in shock.

'Stimulants now, or . . . ?' began Blake.

'Tyler, we have a new guest!' shouted one of the lackeys.

Simon turned to see one of Salazar's men coming up from the stairs with a fearful-looking Rita. She was shaking from head to toe, whimpering beneath the man's gaze. He thrust her forward and she fell to her hands and knees near Simon.

'I'm glad to see not all of you were taken in by the cops,' Tyler grinned.

'Thought she might be a fun addition to the party, seeing as how she's been working with your boy for a while.'

Rita glanced up at Simon, then at the table that stood a few feet away.

Salazar's lackey smirked and pulled out his gun, aiming at Rita.

'And now the fun begins,' he declared.

Simon held his breath as chaos ensued around him before his brain registered what was happening.

Rita flipped the table over in front of her, pulling Simon down with her as Salazar's lackey shot Blake and then Alia in the chest with precision – both went down instantly. Rita pulled out a gun and shot at the other gang members in quick succession.

Tyler hissed and cursed, diving for cover as the man whom Simon thought was Salazar's henchman moved to crouch protectively by Johnny's unconscious form.

Simon gaped at Rita. 'Holy shit, Rita!'

'Sorry, Simon, couldn't tell ya,' said Rita, as she expertly unbound Simon's hands.

Tyler shot back at the other man who ducked and shot back. Tyler moved back behind the wall where he hid.

The other agent pulled Johnny with him to hide behind a couch. He checked his pulse and spoke into an earpiece. 'Detective Miller's still alive but he needs medical attention stat.'

Tyler emerged from behind the wall, shooting their way as he moved to a different hiding spot. Rita shot back at Tyler. She crouched back down and reclipped her gun.

'But Salazar . . . back at the bar,' Simon stammered, still trying to process it all.

'Had to make it legit,' replied Rita, peering over the table, gun ready to fire. She crouched back down and met Simon's gaze. 'I was to protect you should your father ever show his face.' She motioned her head towards the other agent. 'Dimitri was on Salazar.'

A bullet whizzed past just above Simon's head. Dimitri crouch-ran from his hiding spot towards Tyler and rammed his head into his stomach, pushing him to the ground. Rita emerged from behind the table, running towards them, training her gun on Tyler as the man wrestled with Dimitri.

More shots were exchanged, but it seemed all three had missed.

Simon dashed to his brother's body and leaned his back against the couch as gunfire thundered outside the warehouse loft. He took Johnny's hand and held it tightly. He heard Rita scream and there was another shot.

'Agent down! Agent down!' Dimitri cried out.

'No!' shouted Simon. He peered from behind the couch, back still against it. Rita was on the floor where blood was quickly puddling from a gunshot wound to the chest. Then, Tyler shot Dimitri in the stomach. Dimitri placed a hand on his wound, grunting, before dropping his gun and falling to his knees.

Simon quickly whipped back to his hiding position, holding his breath, still gripping Johnny's hand tightly.

Another gunshot tore through the loft followed by the thud of Dimitri's body.

Paralyzed in place, Simon's heart raced in his chest.

He heard heavy steps approach his spot before his father's shadow loomed over the couch.

Simon looked up as Tyler Miller stopped before him and his unconscious brother. Simon heard the clip of the gun as Tyler aimed at his head.

Tyler's gaze was harsh.

'Is this what you've always planned for us, dad?' Simon quavered.

'You sealed your fate the minute you and your mother walked out on me.'

Trembling and unable to urge himself to move, Simon watched Tyler as he stepped forward and pressed his gun to Simon's forehead.

'Goodbye, son.'

Simon shut his eyes tightly. He heard the gunshot thunder through his eardrums. And then nothing.

Then, he no longer felt the gun pressed against him and he heard a thud.

Simon opened his eyes to find Chief Officer Graham standing above his father's body, panting. He looked down at Simon and nodded.

'All clear!' someone shouted.

Simon let out a shaking breath. He was alive.

Graham crouched. 'You hurt?' Simon shook his head. Graham glanced down at Johnny. 'How is he?'

Simon's throat was dry and he had to work his mouth before answering. 'I don't know.'

'We'll get you both to the hospital,' Graham reassured him.

'Rita?' asked Simon.

Graham shook his head solemnly. 'I'm sorry.'

Simon felt his eyes sting and his vision blurred. He brought his brother's hand to his chest as a sob escaped him.

* * *

John opened his eyes to find himself lying in a hospital bed and Simon sitting by his side, holding his hand in a tight and nervous grip.

'So I'm not dead, then?' he asked, trying to sound casual but his voice trembled too much already.

Simon stared at him and both brothers sobbed as Simon wrapped his arms around him.

'Thank you for everything you've done,' Simon whispered tearfully after a while. 'I had no idea the lengths you went through.'

'I did my best.' John looked around as Simon pulled back. 'So, Graham arrived with backup, then?' Simon nodded. 'And mom?'

'On the mend and safe,' Simon reassured him.

John's face contorted in disdain. 'Tyler Miller?'

'Graham took him down,' said Simon. His lip trembled. 'He was going to kill me, Johnny. He was going to kill us.' Simon clenched his jaw and put a hand to his forehead, breathing out a sob but unable to continue, and John understood. Simon bowed his head. 'Rita's dead.'

John drew in a sharp breath. 'I'm sorry. She was a good agent and a trusted colleague. I know she was your friend.'

Simon nodded, weeping silently, eyes shut tight. 'She was amazing. She protected us.'

John nodded and he put his hand on Simon's, wrapping it around their held hands.

John let another moment pass.

'I reckon I'm going to have to stick around for a bit, you know, while I recover,' he said.

'Things are definitely going to be different now,' admitted Simon. 'Without Rita to help me at the bar . . . I could use some help, you know, while you're here.'

John grinned. 'Have you as my boss?'

Simon chuckled mildly through his tears, as did John before wincing.

'Well,' he continued, 'with this wound I've got, I'm going to have to make some changes too. I *will* get back in the field at some point, but maybe I can be more . . . stationary.'

'Just promise me one thing,' began Simon.

'Anything!'

'You keep in touch this time, anytime you have to leave. And you tell me if you're protecting me. No more secrets.'

John smiled. 'I promise.'

Please enjoy this passage from

Sanguine Sincerity

The first book in an ongoing series of
Supernatural LGBTQ Erotic Romance Thriller
books.

THE EXCERPT IS CLEAN.

Warnings:
Strong language, violence and blood.

CHAPTER ONE

Present Day.

The silence was both terrifying and soothing at the same time. Liam closed his eyes and leaned against the brick wall as he stood outside the club. It had been busy, with people dancing, shouting, laughing, all drunkenly. Now, the stillness of the winter night dampened whatever sounds came from the boulevard a few streets down.

This was where he had often stood with Julian after their work shifts, talking, laughing, kissing, and making plans for their future together. But Julian was gone, left before dawn a few nights after they had declared their love for each other, left without a word or explanation. Only a scribble on a sticky note saying, *'I have to leave. I'm sorry.'*

It hurt, it still did, even after all these weeks. Julian had never called or answered Liam's calls or texts after that night; Julian had simply disappeared from Liam's life. Liam didn't understand why – he thought they'd been happy.

He had once relished in the quiet after the bustle of work, now he missed hearing Julian's voice or seeing his smile. His heart broke every day again and again. Yet he continued to stand here in the spot they had made theirs.

Liam couldn't help but wonder if things had moved too fast between them – no, he had declared his love six full months after they'd met and started dating. He was just so confused about it all.

Taking a deep breath, he ensured the club was well locked and began down the dark alley. He didn't want to linger too long. There had been murders in the neighbourhood in recent weeks, all gunshot wounds. The rival gangs were at it again. It hadn't stopped the clubgoers, though. Liam figured it was only a matter of time before both mobs decided they wanted to own the club and took their fight to the neighbouring streets.

Liam heard the screech of tires and shouting not too far. He paused, waiting to make sure it was just some drunk folks, but he tensed when he heard a gunshot pierce the stillness.

Looks like the gang fight's here now, he thought to himself.

He quickened his pace and veered the corner into the next alley and came face to face with the man who had left him.

'Julian!' Liam breathed. He swallowed hard, his heart suddenly drumming in his chest.

'Liam.' Julian hesitated. His blue eyes seemed brighter in the darkness of the night and the light in the alley gave his already pale complexion a blue hue, making his handsome features that much more intense, increasing the yearning and anguish in Liam's heart.

Liam was flooded by a wave of emotions. 'What the hell, Julian?' he shouted, tears stinging his eyes.

Julian winced, chagrined, and Liam saw his eyes sparkle with tears.

'Look,' began Julian, taking a step towards Liam, 'I know I owe you an explanation, I just . . . You need to get out of here. I came to get you to safety.'

Liam took a step back, putting two and two together. 'I know what this is,' he seethed. 'You're with the mafias, aren't you?'

'No, I swear, Liam! I'm not with them,' protested Julian. 'I heard about the Cromwells and Sharpes taking their fight here and I came to warn you. Liam, please.' Julian reached for Liam's hand.

Liam pulled away out of reach. 'A little convenient, isn't it?'

Julian grimaced. 'Liam, I promise you—'

'Promise me? I told you I loved you and then you ran!' shouted Liam, his voice hoarse with heartache. His heart felt tight, and it hurt all over again.

Julian merely gaped at him.

'I thought you loved me too,' Liam wept.

'I do. I do *still* love you,' insisted Julian.

'Then why did you leave?' demanded Liam.

'I had . . . priorities.' He caught himself. 'Sorry, that sounds . . . I had . . . a mission.'

'A mission?' Liam repeated, incredulous. 'Crime mission? Or are you with the cops?'

'None of those,' admitted Julian. 'Look, I promise I'll explain everything. Let's just get out of here, go somewhere safe, and I'll explain everything.' He paused and a tear trickled down his cheek – he wiped it away with the back of his thumb. 'I just ask that you trust me.'

'You left, Julian.' The tightness in Liam's chest squeezed harder. 'You claim you love me but you left – why come back now?'

Julian stared at Liam, eyes pleading. 'I had no choice, something . . . took me away for a while, and I realise I should have told you then what it was and why that was, because—'

Gunshot thundering too close for comfort interrupted their tearful exchange.

Julian grabbed Liam's hand and began to run, pulling Liam along with him. 'We have to get out of here. I'm not going to let any harm come to you.'

'Oh, how noble!' spat Liam.

Julian spun on Liam, glaring at him. 'I came back as soon as my mission was complete. I always intended to. I just couldn't tell you then and it's . . . difficult to explain, it would be difficult for you to belie—'

With surprising speed, Julian placed his hand in front of Liam and pushed him against the wall, backing up as a bullet whizzed past them.

Liam stared at Julian, mouth agape. 'Thanks.'

Julian took a beat, looking alarmed, before grabbing hold of Liam's hand again and guiding him out of the alley and bolting onto the street. Shouts coming from nearby told them which way *not* to run as they turned onto the next street over, darting as fast as they could.

Some of the mobsters ran onto the street where they were. Julian skidded to a stop, his eyes darting this way and that, looking hypervigilant. He grabbed Liam's arm and pulled him close, turning around as one of the gang members took aim at them. They ducked behind a parked car.

'We're not with the Sharpes!' Julian shouted. Liam noted how Julian had easily recognised that the ones shooting at them were the Cromwells.

In response, the shooter reloaded his gun.

'Shit!' Julian cursed. He looked towards another parked car. 'If we can get ourselves out of this area,' he told Liam, 'then we—'

The window of the car behind which they hid shattered as another shot resounded behind them.

They ran towards the next car, and then towards another building. Another thunderous roar broke the air as more gang members began shooting at each other. Liam and Julian's assailant continued after them and just as they came up to hide in an alcove, a bullet hit Julian with a thud.

He cried out in pain, bringing his hand to his arm.

'Julian!' Liam cried.

Julian closed his eyes, wincing. 'I'll be fine,' he gritted. He looked over at Liam as they leaned against the wall. 'I'm sorry I never told you the truth. I'm sorry

I left – I'm sorry I hurt you. But I swear I love you and I will tell you *everything*. We just need to get to safety.'

Liam nodded. 'You knew they were coming here. I just can't wrap my head around—'

'I found out just hours ago.' Julian looked at his wound, breathing deeply but looking like the pain wasn't as intense now as it was before. 'I got myself here as quickly as I could.'

'You came to . . . warn me . . .' Liam was just so confused. 'Please, tell me if you're part of a gang of some sort.'

'Of some sort,' Julian repeated pensively. 'Not a mafia, no. Not a . . . It's complicated.' Julian pinched his fingers and reached into his wound and pulled out the bullet with nothing more than a small groan. 'I'm good.'

Suddenly, the barrel of a handgun emerged from the corner – the shooter was pointing it straight at Julian's head, his grip on the handgun firm and steady.

Liam froze.

Julian stared the other man in the eyes. 'Big mistake,' he sneered.

With exceptional speed, he grabbed the assailant's arm, pulling and twisting. The Cromwell crony cried out, dropping the gun, and Julian grabbed his neck and twisted hard. The man fell dead on the ground before him.

Liam stared at Julian. 'And you say you're not a cop or with a mob,' he said, unconvinced. He pointed at the dead shooter, his eyes never leaving Julian's. 'Explain that!'

'Not here.'

Julian picked up the dead man's gun and began to run; Liam followed close behind. A car turned onto the street and mobsters began to shoot at anyone who was nearby.

'Fuck!' Julian shouted. Shielding Liam as they continued to run, Julian took aim and began shooting at the mobsters within the vehicle, hitting his mark every time.

'Now I know there's definitely something you're not telling me,' Liam muttered as they ran.

'There is, and I promise I'll tell you,' replied Julian. He secured the clip and aimed afresh, again not missing his target.

Liam's throat and lungs were burning but he pushed forward. They turned another corner as the car behind them crashed into a fence.

Liam stopped before Julian, facing him. 'The truth now, Julian!'

Panting, Julian stared at Liam. 'We need to get away from here,' he insisted.

'I'm not moving until you tell me what's going on.'

Fear flashed in Julian's eyes. 'You're not going to believe me without the full explanation.'

'Then quit stalling and explain already!' demanded Liam.

Julian worked his jaw. 'I'm—'

A deafening gunshot exploded – Liam felt a sharp, burning sensation in his gut, and his knees buckled beneath him as he struggled to stay upright.

'No!' screamed Julian.

He caught Liam before he could hit the ground, gently setting him down. Liam's breath came out syncopated as he realised what had just happened. He screamed in pain – a loud guttural scream – then winced, clenching his jaw.

'No, no, this is what I was trying to prevent,' Julian quavered, opening up Liam's jacket and staring at the wound. 'I can't lose you.'

'Lose me? You left me.'

Julian let out a tearful breath. 'I left on a mission I couldn't tell you about. I'm so sorry, Liam.'

Liam glanced down at his stomach as his blood rapidly drenched his clothes. Seeing it only made his heart pump harder and the blood gush faster, and Liam's breath came out shakily.

Julian pulled Liam close to his chest, picking him up off the ground, and began to run. Liam didn't know if it was the dizziness of blood loss that altered his perceptions but he felt like they were moving a lot faster than was normal. He saw houses whizz by his vision and then trees as they entered the forest. The sounds of guns and shouting mobsters grew distant until, finally, the quiet of the night was all that remained.

Julian placed Liam down on the snow, which quickly turned red from his blood. Julian's jaw was clenched.

The pain Liam felt was immeasurable, yet somehow he couldn't bring himself to scream again, and he was so sweat-soaked from fear, he barely noticed the cold.

'I should never have waited this long to tell you the truth, Liam.' Julian looked down at Liam's wound, his tears dripping onto it.

Liam tried to speak but a mere whimper escaped him as tears stung his eyes.

Julian's voice came out determined yet half-whispered. 'I'm not going to let you die.'

'I think,' Liam winced, his voice laboured, 'it's too late for that.'

'No!' Something flashed in Julian's eyes. Liam lifted a bloodied hand to Julian's face; Julian placed his hand on his. 'I came back because I love you . . . because I owe you the truth. So here is the truth.'

His eyes flashed again and paled, brightening, his pupils becoming as blue as his irises and nearly as pale. He let his mouth hang open, and smoothly his top canines extended. Liam's eyes widened and he gaped at Julian.

'You're a—' he gasped.

'Yes. I can save your life, but tell me no and I won't, as much as that grieves me. I won't force this life on you.'

Liam gritted his teeth as a wave of pain threatened to pull him into unconsciousness. 'Do it!'

Julian leaned down towards him and gently placed his teeth on his skin. He paused. Liam felt Julian's breath on his neck before an intense sting.

He winced, grabbing Julian's arm tightly. He felt Julian's lips wrap around the punctures and the pain eased. As Julian sucked his blood, Liam relaxed in his caress.

Julian kissed Liam's neck tenderly before pulling away. 'It's done,' he said softly.

Liam waited, his body trembling lightly. Then he began to shake, but not from pain, from some sort of power that coursed through his veins. It was a vibration that came from inside of him that he felt gushing through all his veins. In his mouth, Liam felt his eyeteeth extend, and there was a mild prickle in his eyes that he just knew was the same kind of flare he'd seen in Julian's eyes.

Liam looked down at his wound, feeling an uncomfortable sensation. The bullet appeared at the opening of the hole in his stomach and fell out. Then the wound closed and Liam felt himself heal inside his body. It wasn't pleasant but the discomfort quickly passed.

Liam swallowed hard, breathing in deeply. He stared at Julian.

He wasn't sure which of them sprung towards the other first but their lips met and their mouths opened to let the other in, and they kissed fervently. The familiar tingling in Liam's stomach told him how much he loved and wanted Julian.

He pulled away. Julian leaned his forehead on his.

'I am so sorry, Liam, that I never told you the truth.'

'You should have trusted that I'd believe you,' Liam placed his hand on Julian's face, 'that I'd still love you despite who or what you are.' Liam grimaced at the blood he'd smeared on Julian who didn't seem to mind.

Julian kissed Liam again. 'I love you, Liam. I promise I'll never leave your side again.'

Liam let that sink in, realising the implications of this new situation. 'I guess that means we're geared to spend eternity together.'

Julian's lips quirked into a side grin. 'Is that a proposal?'

Liam chuckled, feeling flutters all over his body. 'It is if you want it to be.'

Julian beamed at him, and with his heightened senses Liam could feel the truth and their love reverberate and pulse between them.

Liam pressed a long and ardent kiss to Julian's lips, wrapping his arms around him, deepening the kiss with each passing moment, and his tongue traced his lover's vampiric canines as they hungrily devoured each other's mouths.

Liam drew back and met Julian's gaze. 'You owe me one hell of an explanation.'

Julian let out a small laugh. 'That, I do.'

Julian helped Liam to his feet and he beckoned him to follow. He held out his hand and Liam took it, interlacing their fingers. They walked through the snow in the forest, the silence of the night no longer terrifying Liam, and Julian's voice soothingly cut through the stillness as he began his story.

Also By

Also Written by Eidahs

Sanguine Sincerity
(https://binkyproductions.com/supernaturalromance)

Also Published by Binky Ink

Stardust Destinies I: Variate Facing
Stardust Destinies II: The Drought
(https://binkyproductions.com/stardustdestinies)

Multiple Short Stories on Medium
Soon To Be Published in Book Format
(https://medium.com/@binkyinkwriting)

ABOUT THE AUTHOR

Eidahs is a pseudonym for all mature written works, from thrillers to erotic romance. Eidahs in pronunciation sounds elven in nature, which is why she chose it, to tap into her love of fantasy, a genre that couples well with super-natural and preternatural, dark fantasy, and romance.

Eidahs is also the nickname 'Shadie' backwards, repre-senting the shadow self, innermost desires, and a spectrum of emotions, most notably, passion, sorrow, rage, and delight, which Eidahs loves to incorporate in her writing. Enticing readers and evoking the characters' emotions when she writes has guided her inspiration to spell many short stories on Medium and a series of books under this pen name.

Connect with Binky Ink:

WordPress Website & Blog
      https://binkyproductions.com/binkyinkwriting
Medium – Main Profile
      https://medium.com/@BinkyInkWriting
X (Twitter) https://twitter.com/binkyinkwriting

9 781738 282906